Skateboarding

by Serena Ramsay

PM Nonfiction
part of the Rigby PM Collection

U.S. edition © 2001 Rigby
a division of Reed Elsevier Inc.
1000 Hart Road
Barrington, IL 60010-2627
www.rigby.com

06 05 04 03 02
10 9 8 7 6 5 4 3

Skateboarding
ISBN 0 7635 7459 7

Photographs: Australian Picture Library: Bettmann/Corbis, p 14 (top), John Carnemolla,
p 14 (center), Zefa, p 14 (bottom); The Exploratorium, pp 5 (top, center), 6 (top right);
PhotoDisc, pp 4-25 (background); Drew Ryan Photography, pp 6 (top left, bottom), 25;
© Surfer Publications, p 8, from *SkateBoarder*, Vol. 2, No. 6, 1976, p 42; Bill Thomas,
pp title, contents, 4, 5 (bottom), 7, 9-13, 16-25.
Printed in China by Midas Printing (Asia) Ltd

Contents

1 Skateboard Research

Todd was a huge skateboarding fan. There was just one problem—he didn't have a skateboard of his own.

But today he was in luck. He'd saved enough money to buy his own board. Mom and Dad said they would go with him to the skateboard store when Todd had decided what type of board he wanted.

But Todd really wasn't sure about what type of board he needed. He'd seen lots of different boards in lots of stores. "What was the difference between them?" he wondered. Todd needed to do some research in order to buy the best skateboard for him.

Todd decided to use the Internet to help him choose which skateboard to buy. He found that there was a wide range of boards available. Nearly every board is unique, but most of them are made from Canadian or American maple wood.

Todd discovered that there are two main types of skateboards. The main difference between them is in the weight and width of the board, and the size of the wheels. Wider boards with bigger wheels are used for skating on a **ramp** or in a **bowl**. Narrow boards with light wheels are used for skating on the street.

Some of the boards Todd saw on the Internet had a high curve or **kick-tail** at the back. These boards are used for doing tricks.

One of the websites had a section on skateboards for beginners. Todd learned that these boards are a little shorter and wider than normal boards. They have standard plastic wheels and are ideal for learning to skate.

Todd logged off the Internet and decided that a beginner's board would be best. Now he couldn't wait to get to the store to buy his very own skateboard.

2 Decked Out

Todd and his parents went to a skateboard store. Todd knew exactly which store they would go to because he passed it on his way home from school every day. He always stopped and looked in the window, hoping that one day he would have his own board.

The store was full of the latest skateboards. It also had a big range of safety equipment.

Todd's father pointed to an old poster that showed a skateboarder from years ago. Todd realized how much lighter and wider the boards are today. He noticed that the shape of the boards has changed. The old boards were very flat, but the new boards are curved at the sides and at the ends. He also noticed that the skater was not wearing safety gear.

Skate!

Soon it was time for Todd to choose his own board.
The clerk was very helpful. She showed Todd
a range of boards that would be good for beginners.
There were so many colorful boards to choose from!

Then she showed him the three main parts of a skateboard: the deck, the trucks, and the wheels.

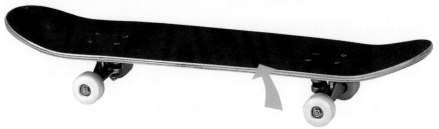

The Deck

This is the top of the board. It is made of thin layers of wood and is covered with "grip tape," which is like sticky sandpaper. This helps your feet grip the board.

The Trucks

These are the metal objects that connect the wheels to the board. The trucks steer the wheels in response to the way the skater moves.

The Wheels

The wheels are made from tough plastic and come in different sizes.

It didn't take Todd long to choose his new skateboard.
He decided on a black board with white wheels.
The board also had a colorful picture underneath it.
The clerk had Todd stand on the board, to check that
the board was the right length and to make sure he felt
comfortable.

In no time at all, Todd was "decked out" with his safety equipment. Finally, Todd was all set and ready to go.

Helmet
protects against head injuries.
Make sure it is the right size and
has an adjustable chin strap.

Elbow pads
protect the
funny bone.

Wrist guards
protect against hand
and wrist injuries.

Knee pads
protect against bumps
and scrapes.

Shoes
protect the feet.
Good solid shoes
help you stop!

3 Skating History

On the way home from the store, Todd spent the last of his money on the latest skateboard magazine. It had lots of pictures of skateboarders doing tricks. It also had a great pull-out section on how skateboarding has changed over the years.

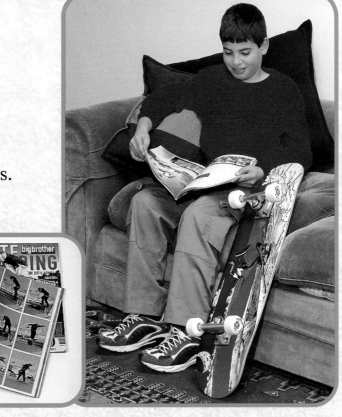

Todd read that, in the 1960s, surfers in California used to skateboard when there was no surf. He also read that there were no ramps or **half-pipes** back then. Skaters didn't wear helmets or pads to prevent injuries, either. In fact, wearing safety equipment was the last thing the skaters thought about. For many young people, using a skateboard was just an easy way of getting around.

Skating Through Time

The 1960s
Where It All Began

- solid wooden boards
- metal wheels – rubber wheels
- sidewalk skating
- no safety gear

The 1970s
The Glory Days

- rubber wheels – plastic wheels
- wooden ramps – half-pipes
- skateparks and competitions
- invention of the **ollie**
- still no safety gear

The 1980s
Decline and Rebirth

- skinny boards
- smaller wheels
- **vert ramps** popular
- **freestyle** skating

The 1990s
Taking It to the Streets

- thinner, lighter boards
- longer **noses** on boards
- harder wheels
- street skating
- skating fashion
- safety gear worn

2000
Skating into the Future

- wider boards
- bigger wheels
- **aerial** tricks
- colorful designs

4 On the Move

At last, Todd put on his safety gear and tried out his new skateboard. He had to figure out whether he was a **regular foot** or a **goofy foot**. His father told him not to worry if he found it difficult to start—just have fun!

Step 1

Stand sideways on the board with one foot over each truck. Choose which foot will be at the front of the board and which foot will be at the back. This will depend on what feels most natural to you.

Step 2

Place your front foot on the board and push yourself along lightly with the other foot. To stop, just put your back foot on the ground again.

Step 3

Practice pushing off, stopping, and pushing off again. Keep your weight centered on the board, and aim for a fast walking pace.

Step 4

Push off, and then put your back foot on the board. Relax and keep your knees slightly bent. Lean forward a little, and push off with your back foot again.

When you feel confident skating in a straight line, you are ready to start turning—or **carving**—the board.

Step 5

With both feet on the board, lean your toes into the direction you want to go. Then lean back a little on your heels to turn the other way.

Step 6

Practice, practice, practice!
When you feel confident with these moves, you'll be ready to start some tricks.

5 Skate-free Zone

Todd and his friends enjoyed going down to the local library to skate after school and on the weekends. There was plenty of space, and the concrete steps in front of the library provided a great place to do tricks. Then one morning, Todd's parents showed him a story in the local newspaper.

— SMITHTOWN GAZETTE —
Local Council to Ban Skateboarders

Skateboarders are already banned from skateboarding in many parts of the downtown area. Now skateboarders are about to be forced off of the Smithtown Library's entrance.

Next month the library will impose a $50 fine on anyone found skateboarding outside the front of the library.

Warning signs will be posted next week, and library staff will hand out warnings to any skateboarder caught in front of the library.

Head Librarian, Ms. Jean Hocking, said that the library had received many complaints about the skateboarders from unhappy library users.

News of the fines did not please many of the skateboarders outside the library yesterday. They said the complaints against them were unfair.

Todd was a little annoyed. His father suggested that Todd write a letter to the paper if he felt the library was being too harsh on the skateboarders. So Todd decided to do just that.

Todd was very pleased and proud to see his letter printed in the paper. But two days later another letter appeared.

Nowhere else for skateboarders to go

I have just begun skateboarding. My friends and I skate at the library because it is a safe place to meet and the area is good for skating. Where else can we go? There are no ramps or pipes nearby and the police won't let us skate on the roads.

The fines are unfair. If I can't skate at the library, where can I skate?

Todd Blakey

Smithtown

Skateboarders, your time is up

So, skateboarders at Smithtown Library think the complaints about their activities are unfair. They gather on the steps and make it hard for people to enter and leave the library.

Wake up, skateboarders! The library is not a good place to skate!

Jean Hocking

Head Librarian

Smithtown Library

6 Petition Pays Off

Todd was very disappointed. It looked like he and his friends would have to find somewhere else to skate.

Then Todd's mother had an idea. She helped Todd and his friends organize a **petition** asking the park district to build a skatepark. Lots of skateboarders and their parents signed the petition.

It was a few weeks before Todd heard anything from the park district. But it was worth the wait. The park district decided that there was a need for a special area for skateboarders. A few months later a new skatepark was built.

So Todd's new skateboard did get plenty of use after all.

Glossary

aerial   a trick performed in mid-air

bowl   a large, concrete hole (similar to a swimming pool) that skateboarders can do stunts on

carving   turning the skateboard

freestyle   performing moves on the board without pressure of competition and without the use of bowls, ramps and pipes

goofy foot   someone who skates with the right foot at the front of the board

half–pipes   a curved ramp that skateboarders can do stunts on

kick–tail   the curved back-end of the board

nose   the front of the board

ollie   a trick jump in which the board sticks to the skateboarder's feet without any help from the hands

petition   a formal written request signed by many people

ramp   a slope made of wood or metal that skateboarders can do stunts on

regular foot   someone who skates with the left foot at the front of the board

vert ramp   the largest and steepest of all skateboard ramps